Lovely Nonsense

Martin Shackerley-Bennett

AuthorHouse™ UK Ltd.
500 Avebury Boulevard
Central Milton Keynes, MK9 2BE
www.authorhouse.co.uk
Phone: 08001974150

© *2009 Martin Shackerley-Bennett. All rights reserved.*

No part of this book may be reproduced, stored in a retrieval system, or transmitted by any means without the written permission of the author.

First published by AuthorHouse 6/8/2009

ISBN: 978-1-4389-5303-8 (sc)

Printed in the United States of America
Bloomington, Indiana

This book is printed on acid-free paper.
Cover art by Mary Richardson.
Illustrated by Sara Brooks.

*Dedicated to
Joanne Solberg*

A Forward

I wasn't going to put in a forward but on encouragement from friends who stated categorically that a book of substance wasn't worth the paper it was written on without an introduction and unable to find anyone who would put themselves forward to write a forward, I have been forced to write my own. Sometimes people of note write forwards but the only notes I receive are from bailiffs and from the cash machine which I believe don't count. I have counted people of note and besides my organist friend I have found I am bereft of such acquaintances. Taking this into account I have put myself forward in opening this fine catalogue of absolute nonsense with perhaps a grain of truth hidden in the verses. Any cleverness is deliberately hidden to safeguard any such insinuation of intellectualism that might be held against me in the future. I want you, the reader, to ignore any stimulating thoughts that you think arise from these bits of nonsense and confine them to the bin of absurdity. The following space is for you to continue my forward in any manner that you think fit. I would feel honoured if a few lines added here or even there are dedicated to the work you have read and so in some manner raise the level of this nonsense beyond the mere commonplace.

Forged Love

Invited to a party
The hammer and the nail
'I'll think I'll be a gentleman'
Said hammer with a frown
'In a long black coat and whiskers
I'll bang upon the door
Pretend I am the rat catcher
Also that I'm poor'
Nail listened quite intently
Hardened by her steel
And spoke to hammer gently
To keep her sex appeal
'I'll go as Mistress Quickly
And say I'm very rich
But all the time I'm dancing
I'll be waiting for the hit
Your weight upon my head
Will meet mine in a kiss
The floor will take my body
As long as you don't miss
I'll be yours truly
Forever and a day
In my wooden coffin
Until my dying day'
Hammer did the business
And kissed her on the head
Before the music stopped
She was well inside her bed
With a sigh of wonder
Hammer looked across the floor
A dozen nails beseeching
That night he kissed twelve more

Just want a piece

Through a toothless grin
Mother in the cupboard
Footsteps on the chair
Nobody listening
To anybodies cares
The world collides with Jupiter
Mushrooms eating tea
Soggy biscuits singing
That's the life for me

Fish Story

The fish and the swan
Swam all at sea
Said the fish to the swan
'Will you marry me?'
Said the swan to the fish
With a tear in her eye
'Come to my bosom
We can only but try'
They were married that day
All in a rush
With a five minute sermon
Intoned by a thrush

To a silent pool
Beyond the reef
The lovers retired
As silent as thieves
Deep in the shadows
They swam ever so tight
When down came a beak
Had the fish with one bite
The fish broke away
And looked at his sweetheart
With nothing to say
The swan raised her wings
And settle right back
'I loved you for dinner
What's wrong with' that?

Daddy's Sweets

Mummy said, 'Go to bed'
Daddy cried
And hit his head
With such a blow
The hammer broke
And from that moment
He never spoke
And in his head
A great big hole
We filled with sweets
So know you know

Someone

In the battlefield of history
With a broken gun
Sits a mighty thinking man
Blood upon his thumb
He puts it on the table map
And smears it on a town
Disappears amongst the rubble
Nothing left is found
His head is like a swirling foot
Beating at a drum
Plagues of silence in the box
No where for him to run
Wrapped in a national flag
God prays upon his fame
Medal pictures on his chest
Burns his immortal flame
Determined by commitment
His focus very small
Puts life into subscriptions
And fires them to the wall
On a plinth of molten gold
Alleluia groans in pain
For every beat there is a time
With someone else's name

A Piece of History

Chamber pot
Chamber pot
Come down from the trees
No one will break you
They just want to pee

Chamber pot
Chamber pot
Hiding in the coal
They don't want to hurt you
But to sit upon your bowl

Chamber pot
Chamber pot
Broken know in two
They didn't mean to smash you
They'll fix you soon with glue

Chamber pot
Chamber pot
Left in the attic all dusty and cold
I don't know why they've forgotten you
Just because you're old

Chamber pot
Chamber pot
Surrounded by the memories
Of bottoms that you've known
A piece of English history that the public have outgrown

Await

Margaret the spider
Alone in a room
Devious weaving
A political doom
Outside the door
The caterpillar waits
Legs in a quiver
Awaiting their fate
Ministerial banquet
Mixed with bad taste
Full of surprises
The time is too late

Beauty

Pornography and Erotica
Went upon a date
When pornography took of his clothes
His body in a state
Erotica took out a knife
And rubbed it on his skin
Took a photo of the mark
And stuffed him in a bin

Fruity Love

Lemon and apple
Danced beneath the moon
Apple was sweet
But lemon was cruel

He wrapped her in rind
And soured her with a kiss
She appealed to his core
But he sucked her to bits

Bitter Tears

A flat headed lemon
Was having a pee
When he splattered an onion
Drinking his tea

Onion was bitter
As his tea grew quite old

The tears that he shed
On the lemon grew mould

The onion went black
And moved to the sea
Whilst lemon downhearted
Passed over to me

Chicken

Brain looked at chicken
Watched her scratch the earth
Furrowed up the landscape
Listened while she cursed
Brain had a vision
A trussed up pale white dread
Lying on a patterned plate
The bird had lost her head
Brain saw another hen
Locked up in the pantry
Stuffed full of hazel nuts
Sliced for someone's fancy
Brain thoughtful for a moment
Changed the current scene
He changed into a cockerel
And now he plants his seed

Don't try this at home

A full tin of fools
Sat amongst the darkness
Eating crew cut dough stools
Whilst filling in a mess
Crabs in Tupper ware
Said they couldn't stay
Flipped over backwards
And rowed themselves away
Nothing said of reason
The sun it did not come
The fools rattled hopefully
A day still to run
Wrapped ideas in plastic
Painted black and blue
Years had passed in buckets
Whilst I thought of you
Thinking taught me nothing
A bed of roses pricked
Thin lines across my body
A penny for a lick

Empty of sand

I knew a man
Called Sam
Who ran and ran
Across time
Until at last he came
Upon his own shadow
Lying in the sand

Excuse

The weather was late
Arrived in a state
With so much to relate
That made the balloon
Because it was June
Pop too soon
But a tap on the ground
Said it was sound
If the lost one was found
When the rain dropped his plate
Deep in the grate
She missed her first date
That shattered the spoon
Who wanted to croon
With the blossoming moon
At the end of her tether
The cow in the heather
Took of her feathers
The weather was sorry
He had dined out on curry
So moved in a hurry
And the rattle of air
Decidedly rare
Would soon disappear

Framed

Painted ladies
In ivory white
Swum in the breeze
Of a cool summer night
Framed at the end
With no where to go
The peeked through the glass
Where out side it snowed

Brother Tell

Every time my brother talked
He rang a little bell
When telling everyone's secret
He always had to yell
I put him in a bucket
And sent it down a well
Covered it in water
And left him there to dwell
Thirty years later
The house I had to sell
I pulled the bucket up
And accidentally fell
Over the parapet
Not feeling very well
Bouncing off the brick work
And landed right in hell
I can hear him tell my story
And the ringing of his bell
Hear the people listening
As he calls me little Nell
Standing up in water
Trapped inside this cell
I pick my brains for lizards
Think off the tales I'll tell

Maggot

Maggot on a shoe string
Watched a place to dine
A thousand hidden entrances
Waiting up in line
Through a magic doorway
Hidden in a drum
He found a mirror image
Of the apple he'd become
Struck by the beauty
Of the rotten core beneath
He reflected on his dinner
Before putting in his teeth

Happens

Camel called the canon
Whispers told the bee
Bought a leaf of golden
And tied it to a tree

Canon sold his daughter
Camel out to sea
Leafy found a paradise
Floating in his tea

Hole

I stole a small hole
To put in a place
Into my pocket
Where it would be safe
The hole overtook me
Until I wasn't there
My space is now empty
Nothing but air

It's true

Chickalee Poo
Got lost in two
Searched for a year
With many a tear
Before he grew
Anew
It's true
As to the other half
I haven't a clue

Key

Key to a locksmith
With a mind in a box
Is how to remember
What to unlock

Large

Fat faced child
Called Obese
Sat eating his chips
In a pan full of grease

Small

Thin faced child
Called Bulimic
Sat vomiting his custard
Cause he couldn't hide it

Leaky

'Rotten luck' said duck
Because his hat
Let in the rain
That spoiled his coat
And soaked his shoes
Which gave him the blues
That chilled his throat
So he could not quack
And said, 'That's a fact'

Load

Podgy was dodgy
On his two pins
His weight was unbalanced
On account of his sins

Listen

No one
Knows
What
No one says
Cause
No one
Cannot speak
No one
Laughs at
No one
Jokes
Cause
No one
Is a freak

Oh!

Uncle Basket shot the air
That tore a strip that wasn't there
Wrapped it in invisible ink
So that death wouldn't stink
Nobody knew where they had been
Or what they saw or have never seen
Walking through a jelly marsh
Life lets you down at the very last

Meeting on time

2.30 and 3.30
Went out upon a date
Saw a lady crying
Across a garden gate
3.30 to 2.30
With a little chime,
'Hit her with a spade
don't take any nonsense
I bet she's into crime.'
2.30 to 3.30
Said within a tick,
'That's a bit extreme
I'll take her to the cinema
Whilst making out real quick
3.30 to 2.30
Worried by the time
Looked through his dial
'What about our love
I thought it was divine
What has she to offer
I thought I was sublime'
2.30 to 3.30
Looked quite fearful
As he quickly passed away
The lady smiled gratefully
And passed the time of day

Money

Penny Rich
To Penny Simple
Take your self a pound
Invest it in the market
Or a house above the town

Penny Simple
To Penny Rich
With a little grin
If I had a pound
I would spend it all on gin

Spelling B

Butterflies and battleships
Settled in a row
Fired a thousand emblems
Paper clips in tow
Crossed the mighty river
Colourful and grey
Danced amongst their thoughts
And lived a perfect day
Summer nights saw their dreaming
Along the woodland banks
Battleflies and buttership
Settled in a tank
When the wind was older
Shipflies on his breath
Took them all to India
And you must spell the rest

Never

Never When
And
Never Was
Had a bloody battle
When Never When
Said to Never Was
'You haven't got the bottle'
Never Was
Killed
Never When
Who never could be still
But
When Never When
Jumped to his feet
Shouting he would never die'
Never Was
Who never spoke
Just poked him in the eye

Nothing Definite

Mirror in the wall of dreams
In a place you have not seen
Flying through the sky a night
Rolling suns wrapped up tight
Coloured images having fun
White washed clouds on the run
Noisy beams swap dirty jokes
In the darkness snorting coke
Orbit planets building views
Whilst endless comets wait in queues
Stardust from the Milky Way
Brings conscious thoughts into play
Creation plays another trick
Particles cannot be fixed

Philosophy can take you only so far

Cat and the flea
Agreed to disagree
On the purpose of life
And what they could see
From the fleas perspective
The cat provided food
For he had plenty of it
Whatever be his mood
The cat saw it differently
Saw him taking blood
Tearing at his flesh
With a bite and a tug
Flea nodded sagely
Looked upon the sky
Said of mother natures mysteries
We can only sigh
Cat squashed the little bastard
As gently as he could
And smiled the smiles of angels
For his own blood tasted good

On its way

A little balloon
With its flies undone
Crooned to the moon
As it passed to the sun

Down

A little balloon
With its flies still undone
Crashed to the earth
With its string in its tongue

Parrot

Parrot said to Turtle
For want of something else
'I'll probably keep my glory
and be stuffed upon a shelf.'
Turtle looked at parrot
And knew the time of day
A figure grey and dusty
With nothing left to say

Slice

A slim slice of ham
With a full skirt made of jam
Flew through the air in a hurry
For a bread on the rye
With a tasty looking tie
Had pumped up her skirts full of curry

Smell

Ginger the cat said
'I smell a rat'

Said Freddie the dog
'I smell a hog'

But Simon the spider
Just farted again

Something or other

On a bed of roses
The fish sipped his tea
Moon slipped his shadow
And fell into the sea
Worm said to purple
Ideas above his head
'In a land of foreign traffic
There's a cracked wall of lead'

Sparrow

Sparrow on a milk top
Read a little book
He pecked at it for ages
Not knowing how to cook

Spider

The spider
Slid down the glass
Came to an end
Upon his arse

Tight

Drunken singing spider
Webbed himself so tight
Thought he was a tailor
But now he's out of sight

Kippered

The Skipper sat in the Nova
Counting out his cares
Beer strained through his socks
As he chewed upon the air
Arthritis wracked his body
His limbs were full of joints
He smoked them on the outside
Rheumy eyed the lottery points
Bells tolled out his fortune
Ships fell about the sea
The skipper sat in the Nova
For the life he could not see
He placed a bet on negative
Doom dark and endless gloom
He crawled inside a packet
And ate the god damned room
But he could tell a story
With laughter in his eye
That rocked the public sideways
And never told a lie
Became a living legend
As tales of his past
Floated down the river
Forty years before the mast

Tea pot scalded Lily

Lily ate the tea pot
When standing up to vote
Startled by a flying bun
She buttoned up her coat
Slipped out of territory
Never seen again
But symbols of her mating
Fell down amongst the rain

More Tea

The chicken and the albatross
Ate watermelon scones for tea
And wondered at the Milky Way

                                    Whilst rat said, 'None for me'.

Tell it as it is

It isn't the colour that
Flies over the sea
Or the rain
That melts in herbal tea
It isn't the draught
That cuts through the ice
Or marshmallow humbugs
Tasting so nice
It isn't the rainbow
Pulling a tune
It isn't the sun
Dressed to play gin
Or a weatherman's nets
Gathering in sin
None of these
Rate such a tease
As the person whose straight
And says what they mean

In one

Millie the Mole
Sunk a deep hole
Right in the middle
Of the green
The caddy expressed
From the depth of his vest
A hole in one
It would seem

Things we do

I went to bed
Instead
Of hanging in a cupboard
In my bed
I felt an awful dread
I'd drowned old Mother Hubbard

Rubbish

Rubbish Rubbish Rubbish
Piled around a tree
A symbol of prosperity
For all the world to see
Blinded by the plastic
Cut up by the cans
Wasted by the lack of air
Her last thoughts were of man
Memories of paradise
Leaves budding in the sun
Of children in her branches
And summer's gentle hum
Her brittle boughs were breaking
But never hit the ground
For amongst the rubbish
Not a living sound
Perhaps she had been dreaming
Though it felt quite strange
To feel the deadness from her roots
As lifeless she became
(Pause)
Rubbish was a gift of life
Revealed that all was plenty
Until it swallowed all our hope
And left the world quite empty

To dine

A man came to dine
But didn't like lamb
Or ham
Didn't like cheeses
Bad for his knees
Had a cow called Keith
So couldn't eat beef
All eggs had legs
And they pissed in the veg
Chicken was off
All fowl was foul
So we gave him a gin
But all drink was sin
We offered dessert
He said that it hurt
So we fed him some dirt
And the grin on his face
Agreed with his taste

Tummy

The back of my tummy
Is really quite funny
Because it is bare
And there's nothing of hair
But it holds up my chest
Which swells out my vest
So we mustn't despair
If growth isn't there

Visit

The eel lined his pockets
With slices of bread
And smoothed out his wrinkles
That furrowed his head
A page at the door
Answered his knock
Thrown by a blind bat
Who lived in a clock
Entering sideways
Played a small tune
And wrote on the page
A moment too soon

Well mannered

The rose blew her nose
On the trunk of a tree
When out flew a tongue
Unable to see
Searched through the air
All covered in slime
Searching for rudeness
To challenge the crime
Rose let go her thorns
In attempt to escape
But slipped on a petal
Into hell's gate
With hardly a lick
Into a world you can't trace
If your manners aren't perfect
Then be doomed to your fate

What do we know?

A man with too many eyes
Caught a surprise
Which he hid in his ears
For fear
Of knowing too much

Words

Forty thousand words
Crammed
Into my brain
Only two of them
Tell me
'I'm insane'

Yummy

Claire had a little girl
Who stood upon her tummy

She tugged her tight every night
And filled her eyes with honey

Every morn before the dawn
Before the sun had caught her

She crystallised her two black eyes
To stop her getting shorter

Lightning Source UK Ltd.
Milton Keynes UK
19 November 2009

146456UK00001BA/82/P